KT-482-798

DISNEY'S

TROUBLE
IN THE
JUNGLE

GROLIER
BOOKS

"This is the life for me!"
said Mowgli the jungle boy.
   Mowgli was riding on
Baloo the bear.
   Baloo was floating in the pond.
   "What a lazy pair you are!"
said Bagheera the panther from
his tree branch.

Suddenly Bagheera pricked up his ears.

A loud noise like a trumpet sounded through the jungle.

It was Hathi, the leader of the elephants.

"Something's wrong!" said Bagheera.

"What's the matter?"
asked Mowgli.
"The elephants are
calling for help,"
said Bagheera.
"Let's go!"
said Baloo.

Mowgli and Baloo followed Bagheera
down the jungle path.

"There is no time to waste," said
Bagheera.

"Don't worry—we're ready for action!"
said Baloo.

Soon the friends
came to a clearing.
Hathi was speaking
to his worried troops.

A mother elephant looked very unhappy.
"What's wrong?" asked Bagheera.
"My baby went off to explore while
I was sleeping," said the elephant.
"We can not find him anywhere. And
he does not answer our calls."
"We'll help you find him," said Baloo.
"Let's think of a plan," said Bagheera.

"I think we should do THIS—" Baloo began.
"Listen to MY plan," said Bagheera.
"No, I have an idea," said Hathi.
All the animals were arguing.
So Mowgli decided to go look for
the baby elephant himself.

Mowgli had grown up
in the jungle.
He was a good scout.
Soon he saw tracks
on the ground.

"These tracks belong to
a baby elephant and a man,"
thought Mowgli.
He did not see Kaa
the snake watching him.

Mowgli quickly followed the tracks
deep into the jungle.

Kaa slid down the tree to follow Mowgli.

But Shere Khan the tiger had also seen
Mowgli.

And Shere Khan wanted the boy for
himself!

The tiger jumped out of the bushes.
He slapped his paw down on Kaa's head.
"That little boy cub is MY dinner!" said
Shere Khan. "I have waited a long time
to catch him. Leave him alone, Kaa!"

Kaa knew when he was beaten.
He glided away with an angry hiss.

Mowgli was busy tracking.
He did not see Shere Khan
behind him.

Soon Mowgli heard noises.
He climbed up a tall tree
to get a better look.
    "Aaargh!" Shere Khan roared.
"There goes my dinner!"
    The tiger went away,
growling.

From his tree Mowgli saw a car
In it were many animals in cag
They had been captured by me
Maybe the baby elephant was
there!

Mowgli waited in the tree
until it was night.

Then Mowgli climbed down
the tree.
The moonlight helped him
find his way to the camp.

The lost baby elephant was tied to a post.
How happy he was to see Mowgli!
"Shh!" said Mowgli. "I am here to rescue you."

Mowgli
quickly untied
the heavy rope.

"Run home as fast as you can," Mowgli said.
"I will free the other animals."

Mowgli quietly went
to the other cages.

He opened the doors to the cages
one by one.

The animals ran away.

Soon only the monkeys' cage was left.

The monkeys were very
excited to be free!
They chattered noisily.
The men in the tent
woke up.
"Oh, no!" said Mowgli.
"Run!" he cried to
the monkeys. "Run!"

The monkeys swung up into the trees.
Mowgli ran toward the big river.
The men from the camp followed him.

Mowgli jumped onto a log.
He used a stick to push off from shore.
The angry men reached the river too late.
Mowgli had floated away.

Mowgli sailed down the river on his log.
Kaa watched the boy pass.
The hungry snake hissed.
Shere Khan watched the boy too.
"Just wait, boy cub!" the tiger growled.
"I'll get you one day!"

The baby elephant reached home at dawn.
The big elephants were still arguing.
"Hello, everyone!" said the baby.

The elephant mother
picked up her baby.
"Where have you
been?" she cried.

"Some men captured me,"
said the baby. "But Mowgli
rescued me from their camp.
He stayed behind to free
the other animals."

"Mowgli is in
the camp?" cried
Bagheera. "Then
he is in danger!"

"There is no time to lose!" said Hathi.
"Forward march! We must find Mowgli!"
All the animals hurried through the jungle.

Soon they met up with
the chattering monkeys.

"Have you seen Mowgli?"
asked Bagheera.

"Mowgli ran away from
the men," said a monkey.
"We saw him sailing down
the river on a log."

"Oh, no!" said
Bagheera. "There's
a big waterfall down
the river. Hurry!"

Mowgli was happy lying on his log.
He thought that he was safe on the river.
He didn't know about the danger ahead!

The log moved faster
and faster.
It was headed right
for the waterfall!

The animals reached the river.
They saw Mowgli in danger.
"Mowgli helped you," Bagheera said to
the monkeys. "Now you must help him!"

The monkeys reached
down from the tree.
They grabbed Mowgli
just before he went
over the waterfall!

They swung him through the air.
Hathi caught Mowgli with his trunk.
"Thank you, thank you!" Mowgli said.
"Glad we could help," said Hathi.

All the animals were happy that
Mowgli was safe.

"Hooray!" called the baby elephant.

"You did a fine job in the camp,"
Bagheera and Baloo said to Mowgli.

"And all of you did a fine job
here at the waterfall!" said Mowgli.

Baloo gave Mowgli a big bear hug.

And the friends went off together
into the jungle.